W9-AQZ-966

# THE SPRING CHICKEN!

By Mary Tillworth

Based on the screenplay
"The Spring Chicken Is Coming!"
by Rodney Stringfellow

Based on the TV series *Bubble Guppies,*
created by Robert Scull and Jonny Belt

Cover illustrated by Sue DiCicco and Steve Talkowski
Interior illustrated by Zachary Trover

Random House 🏠 New York

Spring is in the air!

A bird chirps.

A butterfly
beats its wings.

Tadpoles swim
in the pond.

# We fly a kite.

It is picnic time!

We eat outside.

The warm sun
shines down.

The Spring Chicken
comes today!
We decorate
the stage.
The mayor helps.

The mayor gives
Oona a plant.
She will help it grow.

# We water the plant.

We give the plant
plenty of sun.

The Spring Chicken
is here!
He will say
it is spring
when he sees
a flower bloom!

Oona's plant blooms

into a flower.

The Spring Chicken
sees the flower.
That means
it is spring!
We clap and cheer.

We flap our wings.

"Bawk, bawk, bawk!"

We do
the Spring Chicken dance!

Happy spring!